THE LOVE BUG

Jamie Bryant

Illustrated by Jenae Held

PULON
PRESS

Burkhart Books

All Scripture quotations have been taken from the New King James Version® (NKJV). Copyright ©1982 by Thomas Nelson. Used by permission. All rights reserved.

Printed by Morris Publishing®
3212 East Highway 30 • Kearney, NE 68847
1-800-650-7888

Artwork by Jenae Held

Published by

www.BurkhartBooks.com
Bedford , Texas

in association with

PULON
PRESS

Dedication

This book is dedicated to my nine grandchildren that know how to make my "heart" smile. The joy you continue to bring to my life is greater than I could have ever imagined. I love you, Zoe, Isaiah, Justus, Rhema, Belle, Elizabeth, Judah, Olive and Tucker.

Special Thank You's

To my original illustrator Jenae Held, for her artistry and commitment to see this book to fruition. You caught the "heart" of The Love Bug and brought it to life.

Little Ladybug was resting on a hollow log when she heard laughter coming from a nearby leaf.

"Mama, may I go play with my friends?" she asked.
"Yes, and remember to eat your greens while you're there," her mother said.

"Hello Centipede and Inchworm,"
Little Ladybug said, joining them
on the juicy green leaf.
"Yum, Yum, this is a tasty leaf,"
Inchworm said.
While nibbling, they heard a buzzing noise.

A black and yellow bumblebee appeared
and asked,
"Hey Centipede and Inchworm,
who's your friend?"
"This is Ladybug," Centipede said.
"Ladybug, meet Bumblebee."
"Hello, Bumblebee."

"Buzzzz ... You're not a ladybug.
You don't have black spots,"
Bumblebee said.
"I am too a Ladybug!"
"She sure is,"
Inchworm and Centipede agreed.

"Buzz ... She is not a ladybug!
She's more like a Love Bug ... hee hee.
With those heart shapes, you're a Love Bug!
Buzz ... Love Bug, Love Bug!"
"I am not a Love Bug. I am a Ladybug.
My mom and my dad are ladybugs,
and so am I."

"Your family may be ladybugs,
but you are not. You're a Love Bug!
Buzz ... Love Bug, Love Bug!"
Ladybug did not like being made fun of.
Sadly, she went back to the log
where her mom was.

"What's wrong Little Ladybug?"
her mother asked.
"There's a friend of Centipede and Inchworm
named Bumblebee, and he says
I'm not a ladybug."

"You most certainly are a ladybug!"
her mother exclaimed.
"Why would this bumblebee think you're not a
ladybug?"

"Bumblebee said I was a Love Bug
because I have black heart shapes
instead of black round spots."

"Dear Little Ladybug, it's true that you have black heart shapes and not black spots, but you're still a ladybug.

You are a little different, but still a very special ladybug."
"I don't want to be different," Little Ladybug cried. "And I don't like Bumblebee."

"Bumblebee should not have made fun of you,
and you don't have to like what he said, but
you do need to love him in your heart,"
her mother said.

"Why Mama? Why do I need to love him?"
"Because, Little Ladybug, God wants us to love
others the way He loves us.
God wants us to treat others
the way we want to be treated."
"Even if they say mean things?"
Little Ladybug asked.
"Yes, Little Ladybug."

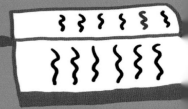

"There are many ways others see
God in our lives.
One of those ways is by our fruit."
"By our fruit?"
Little Ladybug asked.

"Yes," her mother answered.
"But Mama, I don't have any fruit.
I'm a ladybug, not a tree."
"Little Ladybug, I don't mean fruits
like apples and oranges.
The Bible talks about the fruit of the Spirit.
One fruit of the Spirit is love.
By showing others love, even when they don't
deserve it, you let that fruit of the Spirit
grow in you."

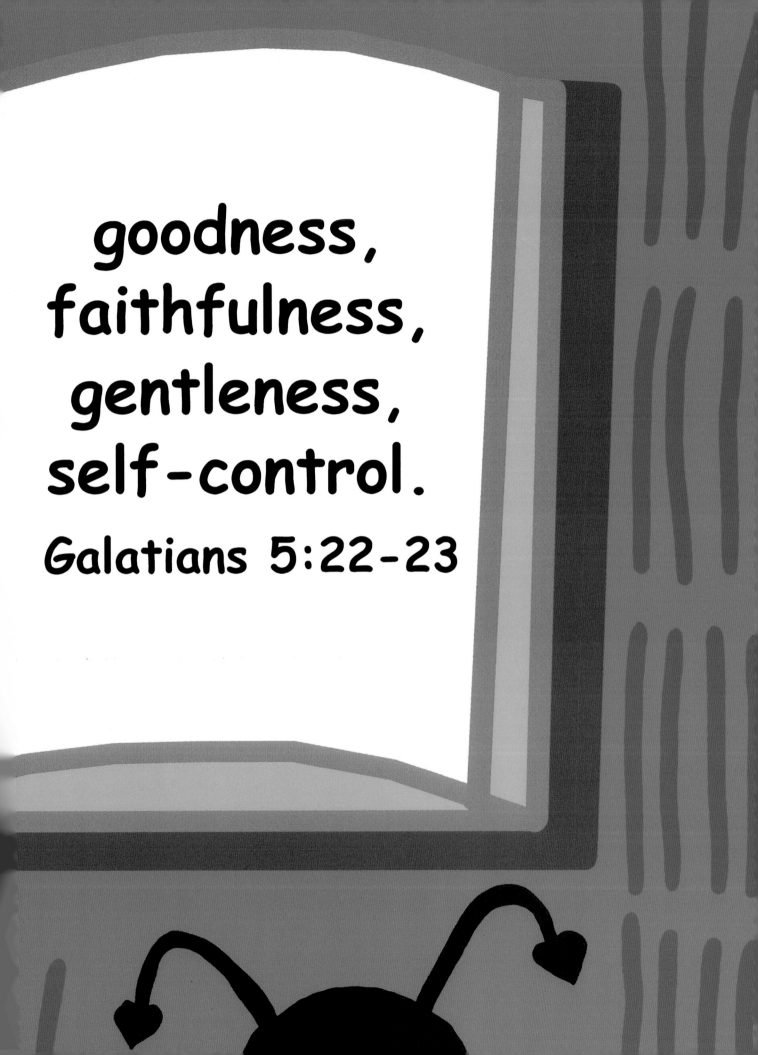

... **love**, joy, peace, longsuffering, kindness, goodness, faithfulness, gentleness, self-control.

Galatians 5:22-23

"If we only love people who love us, have we really done anything special?"

"I guess not," Little Ladybug replied.

"Do you understand now?"

"I think so, Mama. One of the ways I can show others that Jesus is living inside me is to love them, even if they are mean to me."

"That's right, Little Ladybug."

"Mama, I'm going to go tell
my friends about
the fruit of the Spirit love."
"That's a great idea," her mama said.

"Hello Ladybug," Inchworm said.
"We're sorry that Bumblebee
laughed at you."
"It's okay. I'm not sad anymore. My mama told
me that God wants us to show love, even when
somebody makes fun of us,"
Ladybug told her friends.

"Really?" Inchworm asked.
"Yes, if we have the love of God
in our hearts we can show love even
if someone isn't nice to us."

"We're very proud of you, Ladybug,"
her friends agreed.
Ladybug waved goodbye
and knew she had given
her friends something to think about.

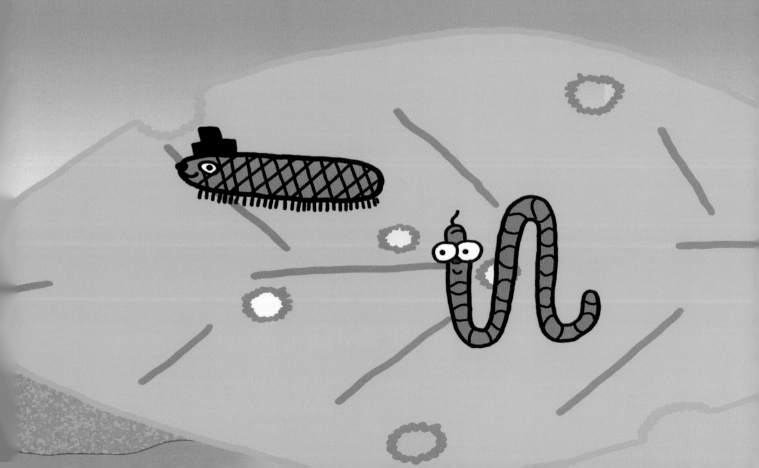

As Ladybug's mother tucked her in to her leaf
bed, she said,
"Mama, I just thought of something funny."

"What's that dear?"
"If Love is a fruit of the Spirit,
and I show Love,
then maybe I am a Love Bug after all."

Both mother and daughter giggled,
as her mama kissed one of her
little ladybug hearts goodnight.

The Hidden Heart

Author, Jamie Bryant, has a tiny heart hidden in each of her books. When the reader finds it, they may email her directly to be entered into the monthly drawing for a free copy of one of her books. The winner of the drawing may choose either print or digital format.

authorjamiebryant@gmail.com

www.jamiebryantbooks.com

About the Author

Jamie Bryant was born in the small town of Richlands, Virginia. She and her husband Dennis have three grown children, and nine grandchildren. They currently reside in Texas. Jamie worked as a Certified Childcare Provider for eighteen years, caring for over one hundred children. The last ten years she has been in the Senior Healthcare Industry as Marketing Director and Executive Director. In 2002 she published a collection of short stories about her life growing up in Virginia, titled "Fish Guts and Other Bedtime Stories." In 2016 she published "Monkey in the Mailbox," Book One in the "Denny's Surprise Day Series." Jamie's writing style brings to life her characters through a child's eyes with humor and sensitivity. Subtle lessons can be learned from her books and short stories, offering parents an opportunity to discuss real-life questions and answers with their children.

f @jamiebryantbooks

🐦 @readjamiebryant

📷 @jamiebryantbooks